STARTING OUT

I0644294

MONSTER TRUCKS

MEG GREVE

CREATIVE EDUCATION • CREATIVE PAPERBACKS

CONT

ENTS

I SEE A MONSTER TRUCK.

They are not really monsters.
They are monster trucks!

They roar,
roll, and
flip.

GRAVE DIGGER
DENNIS ANDERSON
MAX-D
OPTIMA
LINCOLN WELDERS
Coan
MAGNAFLOW
KING
SIMPSON
BKT

READING CORNER

Arnold, Tedd. *Fly Guy Presents: Monster Trucks*. New York: Scholastic Books, 2019.

Gifford, Clive. *Monster Trucks*. Richmond Hill, Ont.: Firefly Books, 2020.

Jensen, Bonnie Rickner. *Go, Go, Monster Trucks!* Emeryville, Calif.: Rockridge Press, 2020.

INDEX

PUBLISHED BY CREATIVE EDUCATION AND CREATIVE PAPERBACKS
P.O. Box 227, Mankato, Minnesota 56002
Creative Education and Creative Paperbacks are imprints of The Creative Company
www.thecreativecompany.us

LIBRARY OF CONGRESS CATALOGING-IN-PUBLICATION DATA
Names: Greve, Meg, author.
Title: Monster trucks / by Meg Greve.
Description: Mankato, Minnesota : Creative Education and Creative Paperbacks, [2025] | Series: Starting out | Includes bibliographical references and index. | Audience: Ages 4-7 | Audience: Grades K-1 | Summary: "Monster trucks will introduce budding book learners to a noisy, colorful world with this new Starting Out title. Colorful photos, labeled diagrams, 'Make a Noise' section, glossary, and more ignite a passion for learning"-- Provided by publisher.
Identifiers: LCCN 2023059481 (print) | LCCN 2023059482 (ebook) | ISBN 9798889891765 (library binding) | ISBN 9781682775615 (paperback) | ISBN 9798889891888 (ebook)
Subjects: LCSH: Monster trucks--Juvenile literature. | CYAC: Monster trucks. | LCGFT: Instructional and educational works.
Classification: LCC TL230.15 .G7445 2025 (print) | LCC TL230.15 (ebook) | DDC 629.223/2--dc23/eng/20240129
LC record available at https://lccn.loc.gov/2023059481
LC ebook record available at https://lccn.loc.gov/2023059482

DESIGN AND PRODUCTION
Design by Rhea Magaro and Jennifer Bowers
Production by Beeline Media and Design
Art direction by Tom Morgan
Printed in the United States of America

PHOTOGRAPHS by Alamy (Peter de Clercq, Gary Mather, ZUMA Press, Michael Doolittle), Dreamstime (Alterfalter), Getty Images (StanRohrer), Shutterstock (freestore 839, Nigel Jarvis, Nerthuz, BW Press, Bohbeh, anan sukprakon)

Grave Digger starts its engine. It pops up in the air. The crowd cheers!

Bigfoot jumps. Bigfoot smashes. Bigfoot races around the track. Nothing can slow it down!

Monster trucks weigh over 10,000 pounds (4,500 kilograms).

Don't worry.
The driver is
safe!

Drivers strap in. They wear a helmet. A roll cage around the truck protects them.

MAKE A NOISE

RUM

RUMM!

Can you make the sounds of a monster truck?

Listen to these sounds:

https://www.youtube.com/watch?v=nvDAql69-WA

Now it is your turn!

MONSTER TRUCK WORDS

engine: the part that uses energy to make a machine go

roll cage: a strong metal frame that surrounds a truck to protect the driver

track: a path to follow during a race